For all inquiries, please contact us at:
info@puppysmiles.org

To see more of our books, visit us at:
www.PuppyDogsAndIceCream.com

THIS BOOK IS GIVEN WITH LOVE...

TO: _____

FROM: _____

Gasira was a tall, extra long-necked giraffe.
For the most part he was happy, and he loved to laugh.
But every so often, he couldn't feel glad...
The other animals teased him and made him feel sad.

Ekon the Elephant would say,
"Gasira, how's the weather up there?"
While Zeda the Zebra would say,
"I think a bird built a nest in your hair."

Lulu the Lion would say,
"I'll bet there's no necklace that fits you."
While Walid the Wildebeest would say,
"How does your brain tell your feet what to do?"

He knew his long neck made him easy to tease,
But the more they did it, it was like a disease.
"Please stop," Gasira would kindly request,
But they kept teasing him though he'd done his best.

He said, "It makes me sad when you treat me this way.
I just want to be accepted when all of us play."
He wished they would stop and start treating him well.
His mother reassured him - "Don't worry. Time will tell..."

"What do you mean?" Gasira asked with his head held low.
"I mean they are still learning. They don't understand or know
How wonderful your neck is! They shouldn't treat you that way.
Someday they'll understand and have something new to say."

But Gasira wasn't sure that he really understood.
He just knew that all this teasing didn't make him feel good.
He wanted to feel proud of his amazing height,
Instead of being told that he was an odd sight.

His neck was unique, but it had its perks.

The others just couldn't appreciate how it works.

If it weren't for the extra few inches, you see,

He wouldn't reach the sweetest fruit at the top of the tree.

Every day Gasira looked for the greenest leaves to eat,
He never tired of them. They were always a treat!
With his long neck and tongue, it made it easy to do.
Even the tallest of branches he could pursue.

Then one week a storm lasted so hard and so long
It flooded the valley because the rain was so strong.
Gasira's tall legs allowed him to stay dry,
Even though the water was getting knee-high.

Suddenly, Gasira heard a loud squealing voice...
A monkey said, "Thank goodness! Now I can rejoice!
Here's a tall and spotted tree that I can climb,
Now I can escape this flood just in time."

As the monkey began to climb, Gasira cleared his throat...
He said, "Sorry to frighten you, but I'm not a tree or a boat!"
The monkey said, "I see that now. I should have known.
I've never seen a tree with beautiful spots of its own."

"Would you please help me? Maya is my name.
I haven't eaten anything since the flood came."
"My name's Gasira. What do you like to eat?"
Maya sighed with relief, "Any fruit would be a treat."

Maya said, "Your neck is so beautiful and long.
I love your gorgeous spots, and you're so strong!"
Gasira smiled wildly as he heard Maya's praise.
It was the best feeling that he'd felt in days!

Gasira kept traveling over the flooded ground.
He was very thankful for the new friend he'd found.
As the skies cleared, they continued to talk.
A friendship blossomed throughout their long walk.

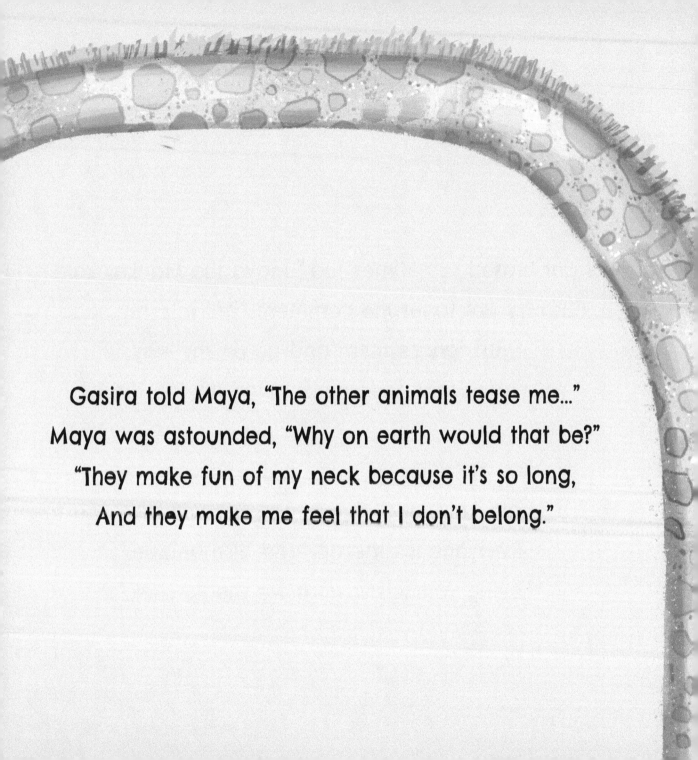

Gasira told Maya, "The other animals tease me..."
Maya was astounded, "Why on earth would that be?"
"They make fun of my neck because it's so long,
And they make me feel that I don't belong."

"I get teased sometimes too," Maya the Monkey said.
"But I try not to let the comments get into my head.
I just ignore them and go on my way.
Your wonderful long neck saved my life today!

You know deep inside just who you are.
You're smart, kind, and giving, and this will take you far.
Everyone is different and also unique.
Loving yourself is what we should seek."

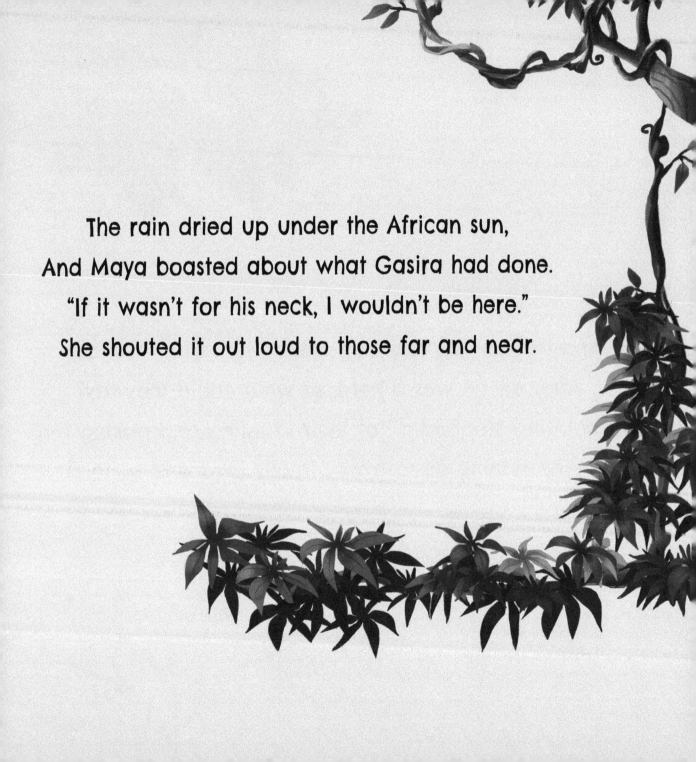

The rain dried up under the African sun,
And Maya boasted about what Gasira had done.
"If it wasn't for his neck, I wouldn't be here."
She shouted it out loud to those far and near.

And the animals stopped teasing him after that day,
After all, he was a hero, so what could they say?
In fact, they stopped all of their taunting and poking fun...
The teasing disease was finally over and done!

Gasira dropped Maya off in front of her tree,
And they both looked into a nearby pool to see...
Two friends who were happy, just as they are.
Their friendship had strengthened them and taken them far.

Gasira had learned to stand his ground and tune out
All the comments that made him feel sad and self-doubt.
He was proud of himself and all that he could do...
He celebrated his uniqueness, and so should you!

Claim your FREE Gift!

 Visit:

PDICBooks.com/Gift

Thank you for purchasing

UNIQUELY YOU

and welcome to the Puppy Dogs & Ice Cream family.
We're certain you're going to love the little gift
we've prepared for you at the website above.

Printed in the USA
CPSIA information can be obtained
at www.ICGtesting.com
LVHW070124291023
762153LV00001B/1